UP FOR THE
CUP!

D. REDMOND

Illustrated by Peter Kavanagh

YOUNG CORGI BOOKS

UP FOR THE CUP!
A YOUNG CORGI BOOK: 0 552 545600 ✓

First publication in Great Britain

PRINTING HISTORY
Young Corgi edition published 1998

Set in 16/20pt Bembo Schoolbook by
Phoenix Typesetting Ilkley, West Yorkshire

Young Corgi Books are published by Transworld Publishers Ltd,
61-63 Uxbridge Road, Ealing, London W5 5SA.
in Australia by Transworld Publishers (Australia) Pty. Ltd,
15-25 Helles Avenue, Moorebank, NSW 2170
and in New Zealand by Transworld Publishers (NZ) Ltd,
3 William Pickering Drive, Albany, Auckland.

Made and printed in Great Britain by
Mackays of Chatham plc, Chatham, Kent.

This was my big chance. I'd been talking about my curving long ball over the wall for weeks and now I had to put my money where my mouth was. My instinct was to rush up to take the kick before nerves engulfed me, but the ref kept me waiting for ages while he moved their wall back ten yards. When he got out of my way and my flight path was clear I thought, "It's now or never." Taking two quick steps, I gave the ball as much top spin as I dared without slicing it . . .

*For Luke Astor,
with love.*

Special thanks to Alastair Unwin

*For Allan (40–nil but
still going strong!)
with love – PK*

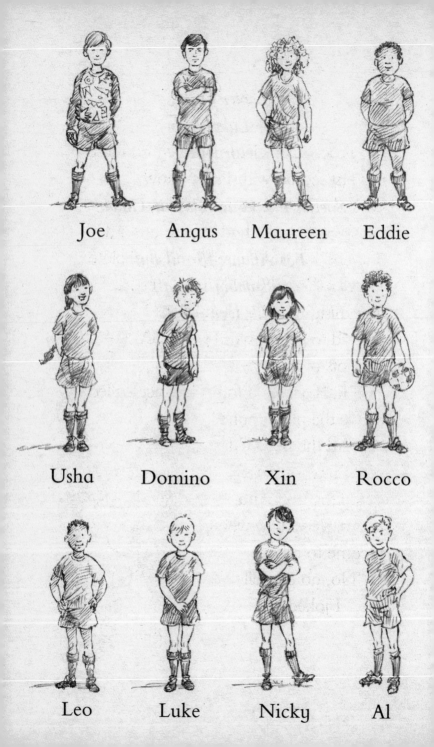

Joe   Angus   Maureen   Eddie

Usha   Domino   Xin   Rocco

Leo   Luke   Nicky   Al

Chapter One

I'm Rocco Angelo, midfielder, and into
my first season with Prickwillow
United. The Christmas holidays were
over, a new term had begun, and I'd
had enough turkey, telly and chocolate
to last me a lifetime! What I needed
that misty January morning as I
hurried to school was FOOTBALL –
and lots of it!

"Hi, Rocco," a familiar voice called
across the playground.
"Heard the news?" It
was Luke, my best
mate, the boy who
knew everything when
it came to gossip.

"No, go on, tell
me," I joked.

Luke dropped a bombshell that wiped the smile clean off my face. "Ayan's been grounded."

"WHAT!" I gasped.

"Grounded," he repeated gloomily.

"He's our main man in midfield!" I spluttered.

"Tell that to his dad," Luke replied. "He says football's turned Ayan's brain soft."

"But he's like greased lightning on the wing," I protested.

"Rocco, read my lips," Luke said patiently. "His dad's talking homework, not football tactics."

"Who cares about homework?"

"Ayan's dad does, for a start," Luke said. "He wants Ayan to go to the same school as his big brother, which means he's got to work his socks off for the next two years."

"You mean he can't ever play again?"

"Ask him yourself," Luke replied, nodding towards Ayan, who was wandering over to us.

"Have you heard?" Ayan asked nervously.

"It's terrible," I commiserated.

"Serious!" he agreed. "My dad went ballistic when he read my end-of-term report. He said I couldn't play in the school team until I'd improved my schoolwork one hundred per cent. He's even arranged monthly progress meetings with Flipperbottom."

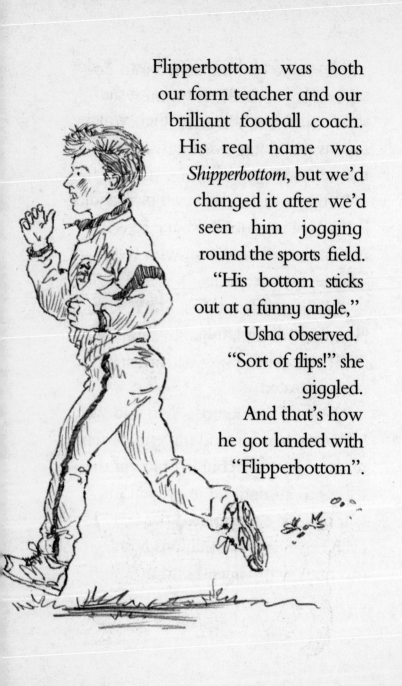

Flipperbottom was both our form teacher and our brilliant football coach. His real name was *Shipperbottom*, but we'd changed it after we'd seen him jogging round the sports field. "His bottom sticks out at a funny angle," Usha observed. "Sort of flips!" she giggled. And that's how he got landed with "Flipperbottom".

Something else happened that day.
A new boy started. His name was
Alan Clare – or Al, as he liked to be
known. He'd just moved to Prickwillow from Suffolk and seemed a bit
at a loose end.

"Do you like football?" I asked.

"Yeah!" he answered with a big
grin.

"Come to our football practice this
afternoon," I said, little realizing what
grief I was setting up for myself.

At three thirty, as we were all scrambling into our tracksuits, Flipperbottom walked into the changing room with a granite-like expression on his normally smiling face.

"You should all have heard about Ayan by now," he started.

We nodded and shuffled uneasily.

"It's bad news for Prickwillow United," Flipperbottom continued. "I'd never have started a school team if I'd thought you were going to upset your parents. I can't afford to lose another player, just like that," he said with a snap of his fingers. "Even though we've got the Inter-Schools Cup games looming, you've got to put work first and football second. UNDERSTAND?"

"Dream on!" I thought, but like the rest I politely answered, "Yes, sir!"

None of us would have argued with Flipperbottom. We all remembered too well what life was like at Prickwillow School before he turned up: a grim world bereft of football. Flipperbottom was our hero. We wouldn't do anything to upset him.

"So what're we going to do about losing Ayan?" asked big Maureen McGuinness.

"We do have a sub," Flipperbottom reminded us.

"Yeah, remember me?" growled Eddie.

Maureen blushed uncomfortably. "Of course," she mumbled.

To be honest we'd all half forgotten Eddie, who'd been sub since we started and had hardly ever played a full game.

"If Eddie plays for Ayan, who will we have as sub?"cried Domino, suddenly panic-stricken.

"You don't usually use one," Eddie pointed out.

The argy-bargy would have gone on all afternoon but Flipperbottom stopped it short by turning to Al and saying, "Join in the practice. If you can hack it you can take over as sub."

 The new boy beamed. "OK," he answered in a confident voice that suggested he could more than hack it!

It was a bitterly cold afternoon with a huge red sun sinking low over the fen.

"Better do some warming-up exercises before you all freeze," said Flipperbottom, springing into action.

First we did some big stretches that loosened up the muscles in our legs, back, neck, arms and shoulders, swiftly followed by twenty press-ups, then a quick jog twice round the field. By the time we started our six-a-side game we were all hot and steaming.

Eddie and Al were in my team and it didn't take long to work out where their strengths lay. Though they both had the same big build they were totally different in their skills and technique.

Eddie was a barger, as Luke and I called the heavy defender type – the sort who came in with crunching tackles and could hack the ball down the field with one big boot. Al's approach was more thoughtful and constructive. He could turn away from an opposing player to give himself the time and space to make scorching pin-point passes and set up another attack.

If any of us had been asked to choose between Al and Eddie as a replacement for Ayan it would *have* to be Al and Eddie knew it. Sensing he was up against serious competition he nearly bust a gut trying to prove himself.

"Well done, Eddie," said Flipperbottom, as we walked off the field covered in mud and sweat. "You'll be playing in defence and Al will be sub."

Eddie sighed with relief. He'd made it into the squad – at last!

Chapter Two

A couple of days later Flipperbottom announced who we'd be playing in the first round of the Inter-Schools Cup game.

"Soham Tigers, away," he told us.

"Soham Tigers!" squeaked Luke. "They won the League a few years ago."

"A few years is a long time in football," said Flipperbottom calmly. "Teams can come and go in a season."

"Like us?" joked Joe, the goalie.

"No, we're here to stay," Flipperbottom answered with a confident smile that made us all feel good. "Check out the squad line-up on the notice board: you'll see I've made a few changes."

My heart started to beat like a drum. Had he moved me?

"Eddie's in defence with Maureen, Angus and Usha. Domino I've pulled up into Ayan's place midfield, with Roc, Xin and Leo."

"Phew!" I thought, as my heartbeat returned to normal. "I'm still in midfield."

"The forwards stay the same," Flipperbottom continued. "We'll have to concentrate hard on those changes during our practice session on Tuesday. And don't forget to tell your parents you'll be home late on Friday. I don't want any other parents getting the hump and grounding vital players in the middle of our first season."

Soham Tigers looked as good as their track record when they ran on to face us that cold Friday afternoon. An easterly wind was whistling across the fen that made my hair stand on end and goose pimples pop up on my skinny arms like purple boils. It was a relief to hear the kick-off whistle blow, though the blood circulating through our bodies didn't do much for our brain power.

20

Within three minutes Soham had scored! They chipped our wall from a free kick and the scramble that followed sent the ball zipping straight through Nicky Chang's legs and into the net.

At the re-start we went on the attack straight away, picking up the pace a bit to try and force the equalizer. The pressure was all on Soham: we gave them no time to settle as we forced them to chase the game. All our hard work soon paid off. After a few minutes Xin brought the ball calmly into the middle of the field, swivelled and sent a left-foot shot crashing into the net from twenty-five yards. Yet another wonder goal from our midfield wonder-girl!

This immediately changed the balance of the game. Soham, who up until then had been playing smoothly and confidently, lost their rhythm and we went for it! They hardly got the ball into our half. We just kept banging it into the area and it was obvious that sooner or later something would have to give. In their growing desperation one of the Soham defenders pulled Luke down on the edge of the area. A direct free kick to us.

This was my big chance. I'd been talking about my curving long ball over the wall for weeks and now I had to put my money where my mouth was. My instinct was to rush up to take the kick before nerves engulfed me, but the ref kept me waiting for ages while he moved their wall back ten yards. When he got out of my way and my flight path was clear I thought, "It's now or never." Taking two quick steps, I gave the ball as much top spin as I dared without slicing it.

It sizzled over the corner of the wall
and dipped into the top right-hand
corner before the goalie even woke
up! Prickwillow United leapt off the
ground like a team of Olympic
gymnasts. I was doing cartwheels
when the half-time whistle blew. 2–1.
Now that was cool!

It wasn't quite so cool when Soham came back for the second half and set about reminding us that they had a reputation to defend. I closed my eyes and groaned out loud as a blinding shot headed for the goal like a homing pigeon, but luck was with us: the ball hit the bar and ping-ponged out! The game went wild after that and the wildest player of all was Eddie. He scurried energetically about, determined to get possession of the ball, which he did with his characteristic crunching tackles.

Sadly, once he had the ball he seemed unable to pass it. 'Boot and run' was his technique, no matter how perfectly we placed ourselves. I groaned out loud as he tried to welly the ball, missing completely.

"NO!" I fumed, but my cry was interrupted by a yell from Eddie as he fell to the ground, clutching his left calf.

"AHHHH!" he bellowed.

"I bet he's pulled a muscle," said Domino.

"No wonder, with all those long balls he's been booting," grumbled Luke.

Flipperbottom's usual dousing with a sponge soaked in freezing cold water didn't restore Eddie. "Al! You're on," he shouted as he helped Eddie hobble off.

The minute Al was on the pitch he zapped us with his energy like an electric charge. He played a hard, tight game and made huge demands on those of us who were beginning to flag. In a flash he had the ball, chipping it across to Luke, who controlled it beautifully with his chest, passing it with breathtaking brilliance right across the goalmouth. Al was onto it like greased lightning, finishing the job with a superb diving header. 3–1, and that's the way it stayed until the final whistle blew. We'd beaten the former League champions in the crucial first round of the cup-tie!

"We'd have lost if it hadn't been for you, Al," Luke said as we walked off.

"Too right," I agreed.

"Well done, Al!"

"Cool."

"Superb."

We all congratulated the new boy, who smiled and looked very pleased with himself.

"Thanks," he said, totally laid back. "No worries!"

They were words I would certainly remember.

Chapter Three

The next few weeks were seriously stressful. My mum was earwigging me all the time about schoolwork.

"Ayan's dad's right," she fumed. "You've all given up on schoolwork in favour of football."

"MUM!" I laughed. "You're talking as if I was a genius. Don't you remember – I've *never* been good at schoolwork! Why are you worrying about it now?"

She stared at me, bug-eyed. I suppose it's not much fun being told your only son's a bit of a waster.

"You'll be proud of me if I become an international football star," I wheedled.

"But you might *not*!"she pointed out. "That's why you've got to try harder at school."

"OK, I'll try,"I said, desperate to bring the conversation to an end. "But don't expect miracles."

"Miracles!" she laughed. "As if I would!"

What with concentrating harder in class and worrying about the early rounds of the cup-tie games, I was a bit preoccupied. It wasn't until Luke said to me, "Have you noticed what a big-head Al is these days?" that I realized the new boy had changed.

As sub he was loud and opinionated, shouting his mouth off and complaining every time any of us made a mistake:

"Get it in, Leo, instead of looking at it!"

"Wake up, Nicky. It's in front of you!"

"Run any slower, Eddie, and you'll fall over."

– just a few examples of the kind of insult he hurled across the pitch during our practice sessions. He went too far when he had a go at Maureen McGuinness. "What a waste of an opportunity!" he hollered when she skyed the ball over the bar.

Maureen was having none of it. She stopped playing, strode over to Al and towered over him, her face hard with anger. "OK, can you do better?"

"Sure," he answered, hardly batting an eyelid.

"Then do it,' she retorted as she pushed him on to the pitch.

Al ran on and got into the game effortlessly, laying on lovely balls as he moved up and down the park.

"Ha!" scoffed Maureen, all set to gloat as Nicky, who had possession of the ball, dummied it neatly around Al's legs. The smile of satisfaction fell from her face as Al cunningly dodged Nicky and had the ball out from under him in no time. Maureen stomped back on to the pitch, muttering under her breath.

"Easy," Al boasted as he swaggered off, smirking.

"The trouble with him," said Eddie, "is, he's good."

"Yeah – and he knows it," snapped Nicky.

33

Our next cup match was against Ely Rovers. It was on the Wednesday before the Friday match that Domino ratted on us.

"I've got to play in the Chess Championships on Friday afternoon," he announced.

"WHAT!!!" we all yelled as if he'd totally lost his marbles. "Forget it. You can't do a stupid thing like that."

"But I have to," Domino protested, going red and very spotty with embarrassment. "I'm the school champion . . . I'm our only hope," he concluded desperately.

"I *don't* believe it!" I screamed. "This is football, Domino. You can't walk out on a cup game, just like that," I said, snapping my fingers hard.

"I'm afraid he has to," Flipperbottom intervened. "He IS the school chess champion, therefore he has to play in the final on Friday afternoon."

"CHESS!" I sneered. "PATHETIC!"

Flipperbottom gave me one of his rare moody looks. "Enough, Rocco," he snapped. "This is a school, not an army camp. Children here work to the best of their abilities in all subjects. That's what we expect."

"But he's good at football," I protested. "He should stick to it and not go letting us all down."

"He's good at chess too," Flipper-bottom pointed out. "And that's what he'll be doing on Friday afternoon. Al will take his place in midfield."

My heart sank like a stone. "Oh, no. Not Rent-a-Gob!" I thought.

Chapter Four

Flipperbottom put Al in midfield with me, Leo and Xin, who'd been appointed captain against Ely. We'd always been fluid in midfield, the engine of the team, industriously passing balls through, running into spaces, knocking fifty-yard balls to the wingers, and every now and again going for glory with twenty-yard hoofers! Heck, we were the heart of Prickwillow United. But I felt outplayed in that match against Ely. Wherever I went Al went, passing and anticipating.

When he scored his first goal I was well choked...

...and his second just took my breath away.

I was jealous, too, of the partnership he and Xin had established, executing nifty one-two's that opened up textbook goal-scoring opportunities. Just to prove their amazing teamwork they scored one apiece in the first half. I *should* have been elated, but I was gutted. I felt totally excluded from the game, pushed out by Al's superior skills.

Flipperbottom sensed my mounting insecurity. "Go for it, Roc!" he urged from the touchline.

I tried my best, running on to Xin's passes, but Al was always there before me. My attempts at laying balls on to him misfired when he constantly moved faster than I anticipated.

"Pathetic," he sneered.

Frustrated and humiliated, I was counting down the minutes to the final whistle. It came just after Al scored his third goal, a stunning overhead volley that I would have died for.

In the changing rooms afterwards everybody was thumping Al on the back.

"Cool!"

"Magic!"

"Wicked!"

Loud words of praise for Al followed me down the corridor as I left school, but I had only one thought in my head: "Come back, Domino, please come back!"

He didn't.

"Domino won the chess competition last night," Flipperbottom announced in Assembly the next morning. "He's the East Anglian schoolboy chess champion," he added, beaming with pride.

"That's Domino out of the frame for ever," I said to Luke later.

"Think positive," said Luke. "He's being replaced by a brill footballer."

"I know."

"With great team skills," Luke insisted.

"I know that too," I growled moodily.

"So what's your problem, Roc?"

"Dunno," I replied and shuffled off to sulk on my own.

I did try thinking positively – all through the practice sessions, with Al telling us what to do and when to do it.

"Come on, Roc, get your boots on the right feet!" he yelled, putting me off my stride and making me fudge my passes.

It wasn't that nobody else yelled during the practice. We all shouted ourselves hoarse but *his* shouting un-nerved me. Instead of following my instincts I doubted myself, dithered and lost the moment. I felt I was on a severe downward spiral and when Flipperbottom appointed Xin captain AGAIN I knew the writing was on the wall.

"Get a grip, Roc," Luke urged.

"WHY?" I raged. "I *know* I'm a failure and now Flipperbottom's confirmed it."

"RUBBISH!" Luke protested. "He tries out different captains all the time."

"Yeah, but this is the second time running that Xin's captained us in a game – and this is a crucial match," I pointed out. "It's a cup-tie qualifier! Don't you think that says something?"

"Listen, Roc," said Luke gently. "You're not a failure; you've just lost the plot a bit."

"What do you mean?"

"You've gone all . . ." He searched around for the right word.

"WHAT?" I demanded impatiently.

"Wobbly," he replied. "As if you can't make your mind up which way to go or what to do with the ball. You never used to be like that," he concluded sadly.

"Thanks!" I snapped and walked off in a huff – but I knew he was right.

Al scored a hat-trick against Wandlebury Wanderers and got us through to the Inter-Schools quarter-finals. Prickwillow United, a team that had been up and running for less than six months, was through to the quarter-finals, thanks to the new player who I couldn't stand!

As we dragged off our muddy boots in the changing rooms I suddenly heard myself ask the question that had been going round in my head for weeks: "How did you get so good at football, Al?"

There was a stunned silence, but what did I care? I'd got nothing to lose.

"My dad taught me," Al replied.

"Your dad!" I laughed. "Is he Gazza or something?"

"No, he's the FA scout for East Anglia," Al replied, cool as a cucumber.

"THE SCOUT FOR EAST ANGLIA!" My words of astonishment echoed around the changing room. "I don't believe you."

Al shrugged as if he didn't care. "Suit yourself," he replied.

"Why didn't he tell us before?" I ranted as Luke and I walked home. "I mean, imagine having a dad who's a football scout."

"My mum knew somebody who had tea with the queen," Luke said, trying hard to impress me.

I gave him a withering look. "That's sad," I answered and we both burst out laughing.

Chapter Five

Spring came in with a whoosh.

"A sign of new hope, life born again," Flipperbottom waxed poetically.

Daffodils in pots, blazing on the classroom windowsill, didn't give me hope. Nothing gave me hope. Now that everybody knew Al's dad was the county scout they were all sucking up to him, trying to get an invite back to his house so that they could meet the local "star".

Al lapped it up, getting more big-headed by the day. He even brought an old photograph album into school and showed us his dad playing for the England youth team.

"Everybody wanted him," Al boasted.

"Oh, yeah?" Eddie asked. "So how come nobody took him?"

"Knee-cap injury," Al answered. The boy was never fazed. He had a smart answer for everything!

"It must be magic having a dad who can teach you all the tricks of the trade," sighed Joe, whose dad was an accountant.

"It's the best," Al smirked.

At our next practice Flipperbottom
had Xin and me doing some close
teamwork together. It was a laugh,
just like the old days, and for the first
time in weeks I felt a surge of
confidence. When Al started yelling
his sarky comments across the park I
was suddenly able to ignore him. In
a rush of confidence I snatched the
ball and made long, bold runs from
deep within the midfield, swerving
balls to Luke and Nicky on the wing.
Confidence breeds confidence, and I
felt it as I forged on, pushing the ball
to the touchline and laying on perfect
crosses.

'Yeah, rock on, Angelo!" cheered Luke, using the old chant that was pure music in my ears.

The last thing I wanted to hear was the whistle. "Pack up now," Flipperbottom called out over our loud protests. "Excellent work, Roc. Superb."

Oh, I was happy that night – and even happier the next morning.

Luke thumped me on the back as I walked into school. "You're captain for the quarter-finals!" he yelled.

"ME!!!" I gasped, going dizzy with surprise. See for yourself," Luke replied.

I ran to the sports notice board and there it was: my name, Rocco Angelo, captain!

"YEAH!!" I shouted, as high as a kite.

"The bad news is we're playing Chittering Chasers," Luke pointed out. "They haven't lost a game all season."

"Well, it's about time they did," I answered with the certainty of a captain who leads a strong team. "We'll slaughter them!"

The afternoon of the quarter-finals d-r-a-g-g-e-d! I couldn't finish my school dinner because of the butterflies dancing in my stomach and I couldn't concentrate on a thing during the afternoon. Maths and science went in one ear and out the other as I watched the clock tick away the hours to three-thirty.

While most of the team were having a light snack I nipped into the changing room to check I'd got all my gear and there I found Al, slumped on a bench. Now you've got to remember that we hadn't really been on speaking terms for weeks. But seeing him sitting there, all hunched up and miserable, I felt unexpectedly anxious.

"What's up?" I asked as I pretended to be looking for something in my sports bag.

"Nothing," he grunted in reply.

As a captain about to lead his team into a quarter-final game I couldn't afford to have one of my players so dejected. Overcoming my own embarrassment I said, "I don't believe you."

Al's head snapped up and he stared at me as if he was going to punch me. Swallowing hard I stared back, waiting for him to say something like, "I can't stand playing with you."

Instead he whipped the carpet from under my feet by blurting out, "I'm scared stiff."

Honestly, if he'd hit me over the head with a cricket bat I couldn't have been more astonished. Al Clare, nervous. Had the world gone mad?

"Stop winding me up," I answered in a jokey kind of way.

"I'm not," he replied with tears in his eyes. "I can't play. I can't go on."

Pole-axed with shock I spluttered, "WHY?"

"It's my dad," Al mumbled. "He's coming to watch the game."

"So are half of Prickwillow!" I said, trying my best to sound light-hearted.

Al hung his head and spoke so

quietly I could hardly hear what he said. "But they're not like my dad. He's a pro and he'll think I'm rubbish."

I sat there, gob-smacked and bug-eyed. Was this the same Al who'd bragged after every game and nearly given me a nervous breakdown?

"I've always been scared of him watching me play," Al continued. "He's brilliant and he expects the same of me . . . but I'm not brilliant," he whispered.

Not brilliant? The boy was overloaded with talent!

"Your dad *must* have seen you play before," I insisted.

"Sure," he replied. "But only in friendlies or knockabouts on the rec. This quarter-final is mega."

I frantically searched around inside

my head, trying to think of *something* I could do or say that would convince Al how much we needed him.

"Listen, we're mates here at Prickwillow. We're a team. We'll look after you," I said, speaking from the heart.

He gave me a long look. "I've been up your nose these last few weeks. Shouting and showing off helped me cover up my real feelings," he confessed.

It was an awkward moment but luckily the changing-room door flew open and the team poured in, cheering and chanting. "WHO-AH! WHO-AH!"

"You can do it, Al," I whispered, shoving his boots into his hands. "We need you. Get dressed."

Chapter Six

I knew immediately who Al's dad was. He looked exactly like Al – big and strong – and sounded like him too, loud and self-opinionated.

"Come on, lad!" he bellowed as soon as Al ran on. "Go for it!"

Instead of flashing his usual confident grin Al kept his head down and avoided eye contact with the crowd of supporters.

"You'll be fine," I whispered as we took the toss.

Luckily we won it, but the minute Xin kicked off I knew we were in for a scorching game.

Chittering Chasers were strong and creative; they had perfected their technique over years, not months. They worked in unison, switching effortlessly into perfectly rehearsed manoeuvres that we simply couldn't match. But we had our qualities too: we were tough, determined and hungry! Xin nipped in between them and sent the ball on a cross to Al, who dithered too long and was dispossessed.

WHAT A WASTE!

My heart sank. We were only two minutes in and Mr Clare was already bad-mouthing his son.

Fortunately Usha took my
mind off him as she snatched
the ball back and sent it down
to Nicky, who dodged the
right back and, keeping the
ball on a good foot, curled it
into the top right-hand corner of the net.
One up and Chittering Chasers were
looking well cheesed off.

Eddie, who'd come on well in the last
few weeks, chased the ball hard in the first
half and gave us two superb chances. Al
and Luke both had an opportunity to shoot
from close range. Luke's low shot bounced
off the goalie's leg and Al's could have been
a winner but for his wretched dad yelling
something stupid like "Blast it, son!"

Al lost his bottle and failed to make
proper contact with the ball, which skyed
over his head.

Grinding his teeth in fury and frustration Al turned to me, fuming. "See what I mean?"

Chittering sensed our moment of weakness and pounced hard. Forging down the park like a sharpened arrowhead they scored the equalizer, leaving us all groaning and Mr Clare complaining bitterly.

"Close the gap, Prickwillow."

"Why doesn't he put a sock in it?" seethed Luke as the half-time whistle went.

"What's up with Al?" asked Flipperbottom.

"Haven't you guessed?" I replied sharply. "His dad never stops telling him what to do."

"I hadn't noticed he was any different from the other mums and dads," Flipperbottom remarked.

"Believe me, he is," I told him. "He's the county scout and Al's scared stiff of failing him. Perhaps you could have a word with him," I suggested.

"Perhaps he could swop with Nicky's dad who's the linesman," said Flipperbottom.

"Anything," I said. "Just get him out of Al's face!"

When we came back on for the second half Flipperbottom was gently steering Mr Clare towards the touchline.

"He's taking over from Nicky's dad," I whispered to Al as the whistle blew.

"Brill!" he said and, with a smile on his face, he took off like a rocket!

It was a bonus for all of us having Mr Clare removed as a spectator. As linesman he had a job to do and we all chilled out and stopped trying to show off every time we passed him. Al badgered Chittering's powerful defenders as he tried everything in the book to get the ball out from under them. By accident rather than good management the ball bounced off Joe and landed near me in enough space to chip it on to Al, who fell onto it, ravenous for goals. His centre–cum–shot was met by a perfect glancing header from Nicky, who sent the ball blazing into the net. 2–1 and Al's dad was looking dazed by the speed of the action. Once again aware of his father's eyes on him, Al was all set to slip back into his shell.

Suddenly a clod of a defender brought him down.

"PENALTY!" yelled Mr Clare so loudly that even the ref looked affronted.

Al stood as far away from the ball as he possibly could to make sure that nobody thought *he* was going to take it. Xin quickly stepped up. Before she'd even started to run up the goalie had moved three yards and he easily pushed her well-placed shot round the post.

"OI, REF!! He moved!" hollered Mr Clare, but the ref pointed to the centre spot, deaf to any complaints – like all refs!

We'd relaxed a bit, being 2–1 up with ten minutes to go, but Chittering were going for it. The ball landed in our penalty area more often than popcorn exploding from a pan but somehow we kept clearing it. And then it happened: the magic moment.

Maureen McGuinness, who closed her eyes every time she headed the ball, by some blind guess headed it out to me. Thinking we could catch Chittering on the break, I turned quickly and dribbled past two of them, hardly noticing they were there. When I looked up I was on the edge of their area and another pair were coming at me. But Al was storming up on the right screaming for the ball. As I slotted it between the two defenders Al ran onto it, nutmegging the goalie as he spread himself. 3–1. We went BANANAS!

"Well done, son!" shouted Mr Clare.

"Watch out!" bellowed Flipperbottom as Chittering came thundering back at us.

They ran us ragged for the last few minutes but when the final whistle went the game was ours. Hugging, jumping, laughing, clapping and cheering – we were delirious.

"You were brilliant, mate," I said to Al as I slapped my palm hard against his.

"Thanks, Roc," he beamed.

His open, honest smile said it all: the battle between us was over.

Flipperbottom was having his hand wrung by Mr Clare.

"Great game," enthused Al's dad.

"Great team!" Flipperbottom replied proudly.

"We're through to the semi-finals," Luke shouted as he punched the air. "THE SEMIS!"

Words failed me, but not for long. I was soon running round the pitch, yelling and cheering with the rest of Prickwillow United. "Up for the CUP!! UP FOR THE CUP!"

We'd come from nowhere but we were on the road to glory!

THE END